Simon & Schuster Books for Young Readers
Simon & Schuster Building
Rockefeller Center
1230 Avenue of the Americas
New York, New York 10020
Copyright © 1992 by Ian Beck

Originally published in Great Britain
by Transworld Publishers Ltd.

Simon & Schuster Books for Young Readers
is a trademark of Simon & Schuster.

Manufactured in Belgium by
Proost International Book Production
10 9 8 7 6 5 4 3 2 1
Library of Congress
Cataloging-in-Publication Data
Beck, Ian.

Emily & the golden acorn / Ian Beck.

p. cm.
Summary: When the great old oak tree
outside her window turns into a sailing ship
during the night, Emily goes on a voyage of
adventure with her brother Jack.
(1. Ships ... Fiction.
2. Brothers and Sisters ... Fiction.)
I. Title. II. Title : Emily and the golden acorn.
PZ7.B380768Em 1992   91-45101   CIP
(E)--dc20

ISBN: 0-671-75979-5

EMILY & The GOLDEN ACORN

* IAN BECK *

Simon & Schuster
Books For Young Readers

Published by Simon & Schuster

New York . London . Toronto . Sydney . Tokyo . Singapore

The oak from this will grow.

* *For Lily* *

Once upon a time there was a great oak tree.
It had grown through many seasons – spring,
summer, autumn and winter – year after year.

   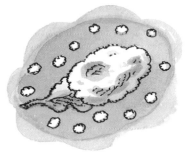

The tree stood in a garden, and next to the garden
was a house, and in the house lived a little girl.
Her name was Emily, and she loved the tree.
She knew that in the tree there was magic.

For Emily and her younger brother, Jack, the tree
was a pirate ship. The trunk was a mast, the
branches were the spars, and the leaves, as they
filled with the warm summer breeze, were the sails.

One afternoon, while a fierce wind blew, their dad came out and said, "I don't think you should be up in that old tree in this weather. It's too dangerous. It might fall down."

That night, before she went to sleep, Emily looked out of her bedroom window at the old tree and made a wish.

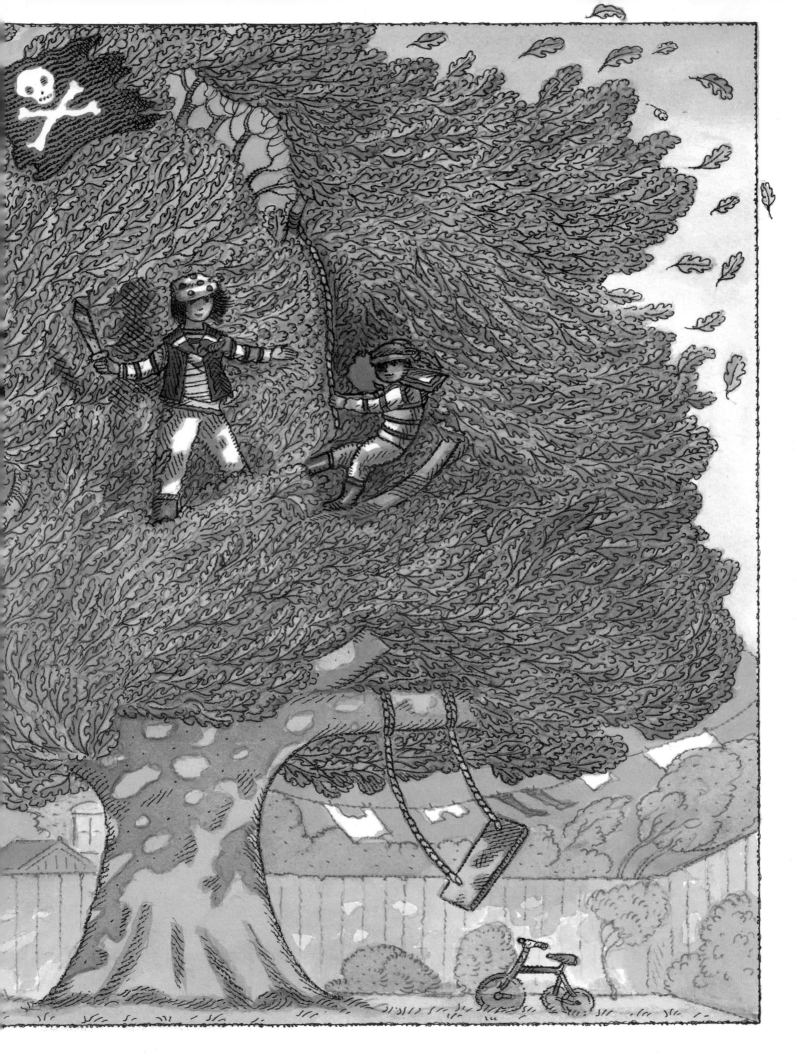

Later, under the full moon, the tree began to change.

The next morning, Emily awoke and looked
out of her window. Something had happened.
Instead of houses and gardens, there was now
a shining sea.

Emily ran to wake Jack, and together they
rowed out to where Emily's tree had stood,
and where now stood a pirate ship, rigged
and ready to sail.

"She's called the Golden Acorn," said Jack. "Anchors aweigh, Master Jack!" Emily cried, and they set sail across the back gardens and into the street. "Morning," said Ted the postman. "Lovely weather for a sail, but they do say there's a storm brewing."

They sailed out through the town, past houses, shops, church spires, factory chimneys and hills, until at last they reached the open sea.

They sailed across an ocean as blue as crystal, and a dolphin swam with them, leaping and laughing in the sparkling waves. They saw far-off islands, a whale, and many wonderful things. Then, far away on the horizon, they spied a golden light.

The golden light came from a tiny tree perched on top of a towering black rock. Emily could see dark storm clouds looming all around it.

"Set sail for the light, Master Jack!" Emily cried, but the strong wind was already blowing them there.

As they drew closer to the rock, the ship began to pitch and roll in the heavy seas.

Emily climbed the mainmast, while the wind and sea raged around her. Jack threw the iron anchor to make fast the ship to the black rock.

The Golden Acorn heaved in the great swell and, just as the anchor struck the rock, a huge wave crashed against the ship and covered Jack completely.

Emily was sure they had reached the edge of the world. She looked down and saw where the sea fell away to a storming, bottomless chasm! "The light on the tree is a golden acorn," Emily yelled against the wind, but there was no reply. There was NO JACK! The wave had swept him away.

Emily picked the golden acorn from the branch.

Its golden light fell over the dark sea. *No Jack!*

She clambered down the mast. *No Jack!*

She rushed to the other side of the ship. *No Jack!*

Suddenly the wind changed. The ship strained against the rope.

If the rope broke, how would she save Jack?

Then above the roar of the storm, she heard a cry: "Emily! Emily!"

It was Jack, riding on the back of the dolphin!

No sooner had Jack climbed the ladder to safety, than the anchor rope snapped, and the wind began to blow them back, back, back from the edge of the world.

They sailed on until Jack saw a light in the distance.
It was their bedroom window. They were nearly
home. They waved goodbye to the laughing dolphin.
A last great wave flung them into their garden,
and the ship came to rest. Emily held on tightly
to the golden acorn.

When the weather cleared, they found that
the old oak tree had blown down.

Later, Emily gave her dad the golden acorn.
"It's treasure," she said, "from the edge of the
world." "It's a treasure indeed," said her dad.
They planted the acorn where the old tree had
stood. Soon a new tree would begin to grow.

The oak tree was consecrated
to the god of thunder because
* oaks are more likely to be *
struck by lightning than
any other tree
*